I0831828

A HISTORY OF FEAR: SCREENPLAY

By Karl Smith

Published by orphic house
* UNITED KINGDOM *

A HISTORY OF FEAR: SCREENPLAY

First published in Great Britain
by Orphic House
95 Longhirst, Middlesbrough TS8 0TD

Creative director: Karl Peter Smith

First Edition-Hardback with dust Jacket-January 2011

Writers Guild of America, west, Inc.
A HISTORY OF FEAR
By KARL PETER SMITH - writer
Registration #: 1251824
Effective Date: 02/04/08

Library of Congress
United States Copyright Office
101 Independence Avenue SE
Washington, DC 20559-6000
Registration Number: PA 1-607-940
Effective date of registration: August 28, 2008
Performing Arts title: Purge the Soul

The British Library
Legal Deposit Office
Boston Spa, Wetherby
West Yorkshire
LS23 7BY
Deposit: January 2011

Orphic House

British Library Cataloguing in Publication Data

Smith, Karl Peter.
A history of fear : screenplay.
1. Teddy bears--Juvenile drama. 2. Titanic (Steamship)--Juvenile drama. 3. Carpathia (Ship)--Juvenile drama.
4. Auschwitz (Concentration camp)--Juvenile drama.
5. Young adult drama, English.
I. Title
822.9'2-dc22

ISBN-13: 978-0-9566156-9-5

Also available in PAPERBACK
ISBN-13: 978-0-9566156-3-3

DOWNLOAD
www.lulu.com

'Encourage the turning of a page.'
- Orphic House

Brief script reading refresher...

Location line:

- **INT.** (interior) or **EXT.** (exterior)
- Locations are always listed from **LARGER** to **SMALLER.**
- **DAY** or **NIGHT** (other times like **DAWN** are unnecessary).
- **DAYDREAM** or **1900's** can help a reader visualise.

Description:

- **Describe the environment in the present tense.**
- **Movement** and **actions** of actors.
- Possibly a point-of-view **POV** specific to one character.
- An actor's first appearance is **CAPITALIZED** with a **(micro description).**

Character name:

- Always CAPITALIZED when followed by dialogue.
- Multiple names appearing on the same line means **actors talk together.**

Dialogue:

- **(parenthicals)** guidelines for the unobvious delivery of dialogue.
- (...) three dots **(ellipsis)** OR **(beat)** a **pause** the length of a drum beat.

.....If only they could talk!

remembers "Dad gallantly wandered over to the rock and saved Ted". This was just the beginning of a long and happy friendship. Helen grew up to become a professional dancer appearing in such shows as The Black & White Minstrel Show and travelling as far as Paris, Australia and New Zealand. Ted went everywhere with her and graced Helen's dressing table in all of these exotic locations.

It seems that when it was time for Helen and Ted to part company, Ted was not short of loving homes to go to. Dean Fought off tough competition to become the new owner of Ted and he seems to have settled in too!

Had it not been for Helen's keen eye and her fathers help, Ted would never have been. Since being rescued, he has given pleasure to lots of people all over the world and will continue to do so in Deans Collection.

It just goes to show that condition is sometimes not quite as important as character and provenance. If you have any stories about a rescued bear we would love to hear from you. Please send your stories to:

Club Secretary,
Merrythought Ltd,
Ironbridge, Telford,
Shropshire, TF8 7NJ

A remarkable true story . . .

From: Newsletter Issue 32 *pages 12/13*

Bear With A Story.

It was quite a long time ago I was told about a bedraggled Cheeky bear who had been sold for quite a high sum at Vectis Auctions. I tried to find out more but to no avail as the sale had passed. A few weeks later my memory was jogged when a Mr Dean Howard called me and told me about his latest purchase, a rather charming if not a little well loved Cheeky bear. I made the connection and realised that Dean had been the infamous bidder.

What I think took people by surprise, was the high amount paid for a bear that would not conventionally seem attractive to collectors who often put condition at the top of their list. When Dean contacted me he said that there was just something about the Cheeky that appealed to him. When I finally got his photos, I had to agree. He really has the cheekiest little face and his down turned snout and happy eyes make him a real character bear.

But this bear has a remarkable story. In the late 1950's a little girl named Helen Shepley was playing on a beach in Hayle, Cornwall with her two sisters. When Helen and her sister were called away from the beach for their lunch, Helen saw a small object sat on a rock part submerged in seawater. The object on closer inspection, showed this to be an abandoned Teddy Bear. The little abandoned bear was in danger of being washed out to sea. Helen

A HISTORY OF FEAR

SCREENPLAY

- original cover design based on *Helen Shepley's* 'Cheeky Bear' story -

SCREEENPLAY

WRITTEN BY

karl smith

"Tell me, is the red handwriting an ambigram?
I read clearly: Anhjah and Golyat."

- Gladys Luna Hallo
Quito, Ecuador

Cover design by Karl Smith

Golyat — **The Hebrew word for 'giant'.**

Anhjah — **In the Almoravid empire the anhjah clan was know for it's religious zeal; with enterprise they built an empire.**

A rare fluke caused by the use of 'Dali' font.

SPECIAL ACKNOWLEDGEMENTS

Special thanks to

Odette Henderson

(Margate, KwaZulu-Natal, South Africa)

Residence: Manhattan, New York City.

"RAYA BAUMMANN"

(1936 - 1945 Berlin, Germany)

Cover design Karl Smith.

FADE IN: lurid dream... present day

INT. LOS ANGELES GLENDALE GALLERIA NIGHT (HALLOWEEN)

SHRILL intruder ALARM echoes through the indoor Mall.

Enter TWO MARKSMEN over broken glass.

Menacing animatronic diorama; NAZI-ZOMBIES flaying their arms contrast with a seven-foot patchwork BEAR.

ALARM SQUEAKS to a halt... ZOMBIES freeze motionless.

MARKSMAN #1 closes; flits his MP5 towards the sound of a trumpet-like horn; a low note from amongst the Zombies.

MARKSMAN #1
Armed Officers! Put your hands above your head.
(beat)
Golyat? Which one is he? The buck stops here Golyat.

MARKSMAN #2
Could be anywhere. Bring the girl.

Enter MOMMA and her quiet daughter RAYA (young) naïvely brave with Arian blonde ponytail; too quiet.

RAYA
We've come to help you Golyat. To make everything better.
(breaking calm persona)
Don't let them get you Golyat they know your secret!

Momma pulls Raya.

RAYA
They're trying to end it Golyat! Run, run for your life!

Bear blinks.

MARKSMAN #2
What the? You in the bear costume, put your hands above your head or we'll shoot.

GOLYAT - 'BEAR'
Mwarh-h-h!

Bear steps through the cordon of Zombies towards Raya.

Marksman #2 lifts TASOR.

RAYA
Golyat! No-o-o!

MARKSMAN #2
I said put your hands above your head now!

RAYA
Golyat!

MARKSMAN #1
Take him down.

The TASOR projectile hits, whines with a crackle of electricity that ignites Bear's fur.

RAYA
N-o-o-o!

Raya kicks out.

Golyat in flames closes.

MARKSMAN #1
Get her out of here!

MARKSMAN #2
He's wearing a vest, take him down!

Marksmen #1 double-taps his MP5, white stuffing erupting from Bear's limbs with every step.

Raya claws Momma's arm: breaking free she falls; Bear falls too; his burning arm reaching out towards Raya.

MARKSMAN #2
Medic!

Momma restrains Raya... still kicking out.

MOMMA
Shhh... Baby it's going to be alright. It'll be alright.

RAYA
They're lying he's not evil mummy.

Extinguisher douses the flames in a powdery fog.

Bear smolders, MARKSMAN #1 prods him with a knife.

MARKSMAN #1
There's no zipper.

RAYA
Don't hurt him!

Cutting Bear open a hand of stuffing falls to the floor.

MARKSMAN #1
Hey, who's the joker?

MARKSMAN #2
You gonna write this up or shall I?

Momma stands over Raya kneeling at Golyat's side.

RAYA
He said he would be my bestest friend… forever.

MOMMA
Forever?

Lifting unburnt fur, Hebrew psalms illuminate the lining.

MOMMA
My god. This is no fairytale.

RAYA
He just wished you'd believe Momma.

Hugging her closer.

MOMMA
I do believe.

Tearfully cupping Raya's blonde ponytail.

MOMMA
I do believe you baby.

An ominous POWDERY FOG supernaturally billows.

SCREAMING BANSHEES emerge and spiral up around one member of SWAT who holds his throat and chokes!

CALMLY FADE TO REALITY
AND THE INTRODUCTION OF THE STORYTELLER

INT. RAYA BAUMMANN'S HOUSE BEDROOM DAY

RAYA BAUMMANN (97) opens her eyes. A medical mask snaps back on an umbilical to the stand beside the bed.

A DIARY lay open in her lap: loose POSTAGE STAMPS act as BOOKMARKS throughout.

Fountain pen in hand she makes an entry *'A History Of Bear'*.

Writing and narrating at the same time.

RAYA BAUMMANN 97 (V.O.)
To those whom I love, there are many things I would like you *all* to remember. I have collected many things in my lifetime; one's which I said I would surrender when the time is right. And I will now keep my promise.
(beat)
You have only ever known me call him 'Bear'. And you will know from this entry that when danger was present, where-ever I would travel, he was always there. And promised to be, forever. Here is the story of... my '*bestest*' friend *Golyat*.

Once upon a time . . .

EXT. PRAGUE LAKE DAY, 1912

CARP appear within concentric circles on the surface.

RAYA (7, a delicate curious child with blonde ponytail) sits with GOLYAT (a seven foot clumsy yet kind-hearted simpleton).

Raya splices a DAISY's stem and passes another through it.

RAYA
Golyat, have you ever made a Daisy chain?

Splitting a stale loaf of bread he shakes his head.

RAYA
It's not that hard; you'll get the hang of it. I'll show you.

She plucks a daisy and presents it to him. Golyat's sausage-like fingers snap the fragile daisy in two.

RAYA
You have to be gentler Golyat. Have mine, I'll start another.

Hands her daisy chain over.

GOLYAT
Yuh?

RAYA
Beautiful things Daisy chains; they're not too hard to make. Try, you'll soon get the hang of it. Daddy says wishes are granted to those who make beautiful things. Daddy says I'm beautiful, because mommy made me.
(to herself)
Daddy says mommy made a wish before she went to heaven.

Golyat plucks a Daisy. Mimicking Raya he pierces the stem with his thumb nail; yet fails several attempts to thread another through the hole.

RAYA

If you make a really beautiful one and leave it on the *WISHING TREE* daddy says that *God* may grant your wish. I like sitting here with you Golyat. I don't know what I would wish for as I already have you. You are my friend, what more could I want?

GOLYAT

Yuh?

Smiling. He successfully threads a DAISY.

GOLYAT

Huh-huh.

RAYA

I knew you could do it. Told you.

Golyat nods.

RAYA'S PAPA (O.S.)

(stern)

Raya?!

The daisy falls to the floor.

RAYA

(panicking)

Daddy's coming. He mustn't see you. Golyat. Hide.

He scuttles away on all fours.

From the undergrowth he sees RAYA'S PAPA lift her off the ground.

RAYA'S PAPA

Girl, look at the state of you. You better not be playing with that dumb-twit... I warn you.

RAYA

No papa, just feeding the fishes.

INT. BAUMANN'S TAILORS DAY

YAHUDI BAUMANN marries a pair of SCISSORS to a ream of material. Of note on his workbench: a pin cushion in the shape of a BEAR.

Enter Golyat with STAINS on his trousers.

YAHUDI
Where've you been son? Have you been to that lake?

Shakes head with a long face.

YAHUDI
Folk don't understand your ways Gol'. They'll make fun.

He cuts through the ream. Golyat lingers.

YAHUDI
You know I won't be able to play for a while, later hey? Go play, and keep out of trouble.

Golyat stands in a dark corner for a long while.

YAHUDI
You wanna watch? Ok, come here, but don't touch, these are razor sharp.

MONTAGE OF YAHUDI AT WORK

He rolls material out onto the bench.

Scissors cut into the ream deftly.

Pieces come together.

Golyat picks up an off-cut. Feels the material against his cheek.

A taught piece of thread snaps from Yahudi's needle.

Golyat maneuvers a thimble between his big fingers.

YAHUDI
What's gotten you interested all of a sudden?

Golyat with NEEDLE and THREAD.

GOLYAT
Daisy chain.

YAHUDI
No son. That's a 'needle' and 'thread'. I suppose I had better start teaching you these things.

Yahudi pulls his coat tight.

Exiting, the door bell chimes.

Golyat lifts the BEAR pin cushion.

He deftly THREADS a NEEDLE...

...then marries two pieces of furry material.

INT. BAUMMANN'S TAILOR'S GOLYAT'S BEDROOM DAY

Golyat laughs at his own reflection in a mirror. A big hairy patchwork mask lowers onto his head.

GOLYAT
Huh-huh-huh.

Standing he resembles a seven-foot BEAR.

GOLYAT
Gr-r-rARHHH!

EXT. LAKE DAY

Raya sits rotating a small tatty-looking bundle of material. She looks to Golyat who sits beside in a full bear costume.

RAYA
It's very soft Gol, but what is it?

His hands mime a blooming flower.

RAYA
Oh it's inside out? That's clever. I can't wait to see Golyat.

Unfolding the material reveals a hand-made patchwork bear.

RAYA
A bear?! This is beautiful Golyat. You made this all for me?

He nods.

GOLYAT
Yuh.

RAYA
You truly are my bestest friend in the whole wide world.

She cradles the little bear.

RAYA
(to bear)
You're my "Little Gol".
(to Golyat)
And you're my "Big Gol".

Puts her arm around Golyat and holds bear close to her heart.

RAYA
Now you'll never have to leave me and I'll never be without you forever.

WEEKS LATER

INT. BAUMANN'S TAILORS NIGHT

A CROWD of rowdy PEASANTS bay at the window. Raya's Papa is one of them.

RAYA'S PAPA
Bring him out here or we'll burn the place down!

Inside, the MAYOR in formal attire presses a scroll into Yahudi's hand.

MAYOR
Yahudi, we've been good friends, sign here, I just may be able to keep the peace.

Yahudi laughs.

MAYOR
They say you're into Witchcraft. That you harbor the *Golem of Prague*.

The ceiling CREAKS unnerving the Mayor.

YAHUDI
They'll say whatever gets them out of ploughing a field.

MAYOR
They're getting out of hand and they want satisfaction.

YAHUDI
You as well as I know the Devil has enough work for their idle hands.

Takes scroll.

YAHUDI
Tell them to go home. I'll sign.

A pouch of coins chinks on the table.

MAYOR
For your time. You are a good man. I need local men to work the fields but they daren't with all this talk of a woodland beast. I have never seen any wrong doings here, but you need to put a shackle on that boy and put and end to this farce.

Yahudi's signs up to "The banishment of the Golem of Prague."

YAHUDI
Just let us be.

Signs "Yahudi Baumann".

YAHUDI
I just wish this many people *baying at my door* were good for business.

EXT. WOODLAND DAY

TWO PEASANT swing cudgels wildly at the undergrowth.

Golyat (bear costume) looks in the direction of the shouting.

SCARRED PEASANT
There he is!

GOLYAT RUNS

Zigzagging evasively through the trees with strangers in tow...

GOLYAT
Raya? Raya? Raya?

ELSEWHERE...

EXT. LUSH FIELD DAY

Raya hums a nursery rhyme and pulls the petals from a daisy... one at a time 'til none remain.

BACK TO THE CHASE...

EXT. LAKE DAY

Golyat, wheezing, goes to ground holding his left arm.

Both peasants strike with their cudgels.

LATER...

Raya stares at the bloodied face of Golyat staring out of a torn mask.

RAYA
Golyat?

Golyat wheezes heavily.

RAYA
Gol?

GOLYAT
Ugh?

RAYA
Are you ok?

She pulls his arm...

RAYA
Get up.

Golyat slumps.

RAYA
Stand Golyat.

Raya swallows hard, braving the tears in her eyes. She tries best she can to pull him to his feet.

RAYA
You're my bestest friend.

Wipes forearm across her nose.

RAYA
I don't want you to go to heaven.
Please Golyat. Please.

Looks to the lake where a Carp feeds.

RAYA
What am I to do?

A concentric circle emanates from a single floating daisy.

SOON LATER

She kisses the open ends of a daisy chain and places it onto the *WISHING TREE*.

With all her strength she rolls Golyat to the water's edge unaware of the menacing presence of the two scary Peasants.

She closes her eyes and mumbles incomprehensively.

The Peasants close in and a wind whips through the trees.

RAYA
Come on. Please move.

Peasants approach within feet.

RAYA
Please god.
(praying)
With all my heart and all my soul and all my strength.

Branches sway, leaves rustle.

RAYA
I wish to be friends forever.

Their faces drain white.

Rising behind Raya in one sharp movement, a behemoth.

GOLYAT
MWARGH!

RAYA BAUMMANN 97 (V.O.)
(calmly narrating)
A sight so frightening that the fields around the lake would lay fallow for many years to come.

FLASH FORWARD PRESENT DAY...

EXT. COAST ROAD AUCTION HOUSE TRUCK (TRAVELING) NIGHT

Rain patters against the windshield.

PIRATE (handsome 40-ish father) chews gum: an umbilical from the dash' snakes to the CB in his hand.

PIRATE
Thanks for the heads-up. Thanks for keeping an eye on my Rebecca.

MAY WEST (O.S.)
(filtered husky voice)
That's the pleasure I get in teaching your daughter; it's my pleasure. The girl's settling in just fine. History is the only lesson where there's more to teach each day.

PIRATE
Some say nostalgia isn't what it used to be.

MAY WEST (O.S.)
Sure, huh.

PIRATE
So you're the infamous May West?

MAY WEST (O.S.)
It's actually Miss West. That's my name, but one time someone misheard and the name just stuck. Plus, parents of the feistiest students eventually *"Come up and see me sometime"*. Over.

PIRATE
Quality.

WHITE NOISE dominates the airwave. He looks out to the high trees framing the road.

PIRATE
Signal's breaking up.

INT. MISS WEST'S APARTMENT NIGHT

MISS WEST (a voluptuous confident spinster) holds a retro 50's microphone from which emits WHITE NOISE.

PIRATE (O.S.)
(filtered)
May West, you still there?

MAY WEST
Receiving. Must be the coast road.

She moves the radio dial back and forth across a frequency.

MAY WEST
You must have hit the--

PIRATE (O.S.)
--I've just hit the Coast road!

EXT. COAST ROAD TRUCK (TRAVELING) NIGHT

Rain beats down. Pirate pounds the wheel.

PIRATE
Ah just great! It's chucking it down. One minute babe, better report in. Looks like one serious weather-front moving in. Over.

Adjusts radio dial and a stronger signal makes him jump!

HAROLD BRIDE (O.S.)
(filtered)
Mayday! Mayday!

With a serious face he peers through trees to the coast.

HAROLD BRIDE (O.S.)
(filtered)
Mayday. I repeat, please send all available help.

He slows and looks out over the choppy sea.

RADIO D.J. (O.S.)
(filtered)
This Marconi dramatization of the infamous Titanic catastrophe continues after the break.

He turns the dial and shakes his head.

PIRATE
What a drama, you got me.

A yellow note-it on the dash reads “CARIBBEAN MOMMA 105”. He spins the dial and matches the frequency.

PIRATE
One zero five.
(authoritive)
‘Pirate’ to ‘Caribbean momma’ come on in good momma.

CARIBBEAN MOMMA (O.S.)
(filtered)
You’re a bit foggy Pirate, This is Caribbean Momma, come on in, over.

PIRATE
Scallywags are falling, put the baby chicks on hold, salvage whatever you can, returning to port full sails heading for home, over.

INT. BAUMANN HOME KITCHEN NIGHT

MOMMA (30’s) with CB receiver under her chin and tossing pancakes with the other. REBECCA (mid-teens) fights over a pot of honey with her younger sister ALIZA (7 petite).

MOMMA
Your baby chicks are getting hot under the collar. Over

PIRATE IS FATHER (O.S.)
(filtered)
Got a weather front closing. Over.

MOMMA
Your little red-faced riding hoods are missing you.
(to daughters)
Waffles, then bed!

ALIZA
(toothless lisp)
But ma'am.

FATHER (O.S.)
Bed sounds good to me.

ALIZA
But I still have over an hour. OH-h-h!!!

MOMMA
Waffles, bath then bed. Any time left from sixty minutes and your father may just read you a bedtime story. If you're good.

Aliza rushes off.

FATHER (O.S.)
(flirting)
Daddy's plans for momma may just take up more than sixty minutes.

MOMMA
Get yourself home you scallywag Momma's getting hot under the apron.

INT. ALIZA'S BEDROOM NIGHT

Wet haired Aliza lay snug in bed. She pulls a PLUSH BLACK CAT comforter closer. A half eaten pancake lay on the plate atop her covers.

Father finishes off the *pancake*.

FATHER
(whispering)
Waste not want not.

He tip-toes to a bright AQUARIUM and dims its light.

The fairytale book 'THE GOLEM OF PRAGUE' rests on the windowsill. He draws the curtains in around a Full-Moon.

ALIZA
(toothless lisp)
Daddy?

FATHER
Oh. I thought you were asleep?

ALIZA
I'm as sleepy as a Billy-Goat.

FATHER
And I've been working as hard as a Troll.

He stomps on his way to her bed and lifts her eyelids.

She laughs.

FATHER
(intimidating)
I see a Billy-Goat. And if you try to cross my bridge, you know what ya gonna get. And you know what ya gotta give me to avoid it?
(softer)
Me being a big Troll an' all.

Tucks her in.

He reaches around under her pillow.

FATHER
Where's my money? So the Tooth Fairy's not been yet eh? Well this little Billy-Goat'll have to pay up in full if your School Bus wishes to cross in the morning.
(beat)
So when daddy has to pay a toll on the Troll Bridge it's so that children like yourself can sleep safe at night, for the Council Troll sits counting daddy's money.
Muhahah!

ALIZA
(toothless lisp)
Miss. Ingle said the money went to the Council to build new roads.

FATHER
(breaking persona)
She-did did-she? I'll have to have a word with Miss. Ingle, she'll get a big nose telling tall tales like that. If her teeth are as big as her NOSE the tooth fairy will have to bring her a BIG BAG of money if I were to knock them all out. Who'd be laughing then?

ALIZA
Mr. Hoffman the Dentist; because he's just put the fees up for extractions and aftercare.

FATHER
This is what it's come down to huh? Little Piggy is looking after yours.

On the bedside table rests a bloody tissue at the foot of a porcelain Piggy bank.

Father unwraps the tissue and reveals Aliza's bloody tooth. He drops it inside a small pill box; rattles it, and with a kiss slides it beneath her pillow.

ALIZA
I hope the Tooth Fairy doesn't forget me as that one's a *whopper*.

FATHER
Certainly a *whopper*. I can vouch the good fairy liking this one.

Kissing her head she gives a toothy grin.

ALIZA
Daddy? If Trolls lose their fangs, do they get more money?

FATHER
I'll have to think overnight about that one, and if my 'Dream Fairy' hasn't given me an answer by morning I'd think about asking Miss. Ingle if I were you.

ALIZA
Do you think *my* Dream Fairy and *your* Dream Fairy are friends?

FATHER
I would have thought so. Just how many Fairies do you know around here? Maybe they're related.

ALIZA
Like cousins?

FATHER
Maybe brother and sister: at *least* cousins! Goodnight sweetheart.

He ruffles her hair.

ALIZA
Sweet dreams.

FATHER
Sweet dreams.

MOMENTS LATER

INT. KITCHEN NIGHT

Momma slices sandwiches into triangles and fills Aliza's lunchbox. Father snuggles up behind, both hands to her waist.

MOMMA
Easy tiger, be a good daddy.

She pops a cherry into his mouth.

FATHER
All the food groups I see.

MOMMA
And a wholesome diet of tall tales.

Letting go...

FATHER
You won't believe Miss. Ingle has blown my Troll story.

MOMMA
Yeah?

FATHER
Aliza only knows the Council are taking money to pay for new roads!

MOMMA
Oh dear, she's growing up fast.

FATHER
Watch me have a face-off at the next parent/governor board meeting.

He juggles an apple from the fruit bowl.

MOMMA
Who's got your back, Santa?

He slides his hands back around her waist.

FATHER
I was hoping me and a little Elvin tooth fairy. Remember that little number?

She pops a SPLIT CHERRY on his nose and licks her teeth.

MOMMA
No one ever forgets Santa's little helper.

FATHER
Christmas just keeps coming earlier each year.

They flash eyebrows, kiss and exchange giggly murmurs.

EXT./INT. ALIZA'S BEDROOM NIGHT

Momma inches open Aliza's door.

The PLUSH BLACK CAT comforter lay snug at Aliza's cheek.

FATHER
I'm a little worried how she's still attached to that tatty cat.

MOMMA
She'll grow out of it.

INT. PARENT's bedroom NIGHT

Split cherry on nose just like Rudolph. He puts his hands on his head mimicking antlers.

FATHER
M-o-o-o.

MOMMA
I don't think Reindeer make a noise. Like that.

FATHER
It's a Moose.

MOMMA
Shhh, you'll wake her.

Momma pats the bed and flashes her eyebrows at Father.

FATHER
(Italian accent)
You no like-a-my-Moose?

He throws the cherry over his shoulder.

MOMMA
Moose or Tiger, I don't mind.

He leaps into bed.

MOMENTS LATER

From beneath the covers, lip smacking kisses and passionate murmurs.

INT. ALIZA'S BEDROOM NIGHT

Aliza sleeps with the BLACK CAT comforter against her cheek.

AT THE AQUARIUM... Bubbles chug from the oxygenating pump and a little FISH swims in front of the AQUARIUM LIGHT creating a tiny shadow which swims across the wall.

The shadow multiplies…

Wisps of writing now swim from right to left from Hebrew into English across her wall.

As long as in the heart, within,
A Jewish soul still yearns,
Our hope is not yet lost.

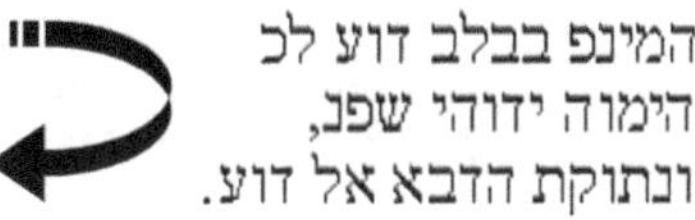

EXT. SUBURB BAUMANN HOME SCHOOL BUS DAY

Lunch box in hand, Aliza boards the "St. Nicholas" bus.

MOMMA
(to Driver)
Morning John.

DRIVER
Morning.

MOMMA
It's a nice day, have a good one.

DRIVER
You too. I try my best.

INT. ALIZA'S BEDROOM DAY

Father picks up the PLUSH BLACK CAT.

FATHER
(as Tweedy Bird)
I did, I did taw a puddy cat. Your days are numbered puddy.

INT. AUCTION HOUSE DAY

A packed-out auction house. A BROCHURE showcasing a PLUSH *"TITANIC BEAR"* rests upon an empty chair.

The AUCTIONEER waves his gavel across a fidgety CROWD.

AUCTIONEER
At the rear! Thirteen thousand nine hundred. Do I hear fourteen?

An USHER holding a telephone to her ear raises a hand.

Attendees gasp.

AUCTIONEER
Do I hear fourteen one? For a very unique hand-made bear, there will never be another like it. Going once, twice; fourteen thousand a second time. Fourteen thousand? Any more for the only bear to survive the fatal voyage. Third and final time. Fourteen thousand?

Bangs gavel. Crowd erupts in applause.

AUCTIONEER
Anonymous phone bidder.

SAME DAY...

INT. KITCHEN DAY

Momma who places fresh groceries on the worktop. She picks up a newspaper with the headline *'TITANIC 14,000 paid for a COLLECTIBLE TOY BEAR'*.

INT. ALIZA'S BEDROOM DAY

Father places a picture of a four funneled ship on top of a glass case containing the TITANIC AUCTION BEAR.

FATHER
(proud)
The best, accept no substitute.

Using the BLACK CAT as a duster he wipes over a finger print on the case.

FATHER
Not many can say they rode that wave.

Enter Momma.

MOMMA
I take it little Miss has a *new* best friend?

EXT. MILKEN COMMUNITY HIGH SCHOOL DAY

Rebecca, light clothing, blonde hair and fresh face.

JOCK a muscular football hunk incoherently mumbles into the ear of his LATEST GIRLFRIEND.

LATEST GIRLFRIEND
(coyly)
Is that a promise?

PASSING...

REBECCA
(under her breath)
Get real.

HUNK
Sure babe, just for you.

Latest girlfriend hugs his arm.

Rebecca rolls her eyes and sighs.

INT. BAUMMANN HOME BATHROOM MIRROR DAY, LATER

CLOSE ON REBECCA'S FACE; her nostrils flare.

REBECCA
Bitch, get off him he's mine!

She coughs, recomposes, and turns her head the other way.

REBECCA
I said, get off him he's mine.
Bitch!

Shakes her head.

REBECCA
(calm persona)
Just aint me.

CLOSE ON: Black hair-dye.

REBECCA
(cliché TV persona)
For that *all-over* gothic look.

Swings her head to the side trying a profile delivery.

REBECCA
For that darker period of your life when you just simply have to get the man you desire before some other bitch does.

Teases her golden blond fringe with a comb.

Rips box hair dye.

REBECCA
So gentlemen preferring blondes? Let's try *bitches*.

20 MINUTES LATER she's blow drying her new darker color.

Twisting her hair into a long rope she compares the style with the good looking *bob-haired* model on the box.

Open scissors crunch down--

REBECCA
Stand aside Marilyn, Jane Russell coming through.

--long black hairs fall into the sink.

LATER

Femme fatale Rebecca stands amidst a pile of dark clothes.

Wearing a three buttoned waistcoat she holds the top button.

REBECCA
Sometimes.

Feeling middle button.

REBECCA
Always.

Bottom button.

REBECCA
Never.

Unbuttons last button.

Runs tongue over lipstick on her teeth.

REBECCA
Good to go.

EXT. MILKEN COMMUNITY HIGH SCHOOL LOCKERS NIGHT

Rebecca in dark clothing and panda-like makeup waltzes the corridors with a tomboyish attitude.

Jock stops whispering in the ear of his LATEST GIRLFRIEND who looks over with dagger-eyes.

REBECCA
Freak.

Rebecca whips a coy glance towards Jock.

REBECCA
'All Hallows Eve' party, will be fun. Do you and your nature-boy surf friends want to get more than sand between your toes?

HUNK
Party? Sure.

Latest-girlfriend thumps his arm.

HUNK
What? It's just a party.
(to Rebecca)
We'll bring a keg.

REBECCA
Wicked.

INT. HISTORY CLASS DAY

Colorful *stamps* illuminate the pages of a Diary in Miss West's hands. She twiddles a pencil into her hair. On the board she writes "Ancestry" followed by a large "?".

Enter a motley bunch of STUDENTS.

Rebecca looks at the board then to a pile of blank paper.

MISS WEST
If you would, please Rebecca.

Rebecca nods and delivers a sheet to every desk.

OBESE WILLIAM (17) smiley yet obsessively obese hums Mendelssohn's "Wedding March" squeezes past Rebecca.

REBECCA
Gross.

Jock takes his seat.

MISS WEST
Definition! Any guesses?

Rebecca pauses with the paper; raises a hand.

MISS WEST
Yes?

REBECCA
Heraldry. Lineage. The study of one's parentage.

MISS WEST
Very good. Almost the perfect dictionary definition.
(beat)
Page thirty-seven of 'Twenty First Century History'. Task three; Your Family Tree. Now some of us have big families--

A ripple of laughter breaks out around William.

MISS WEST
Not in that sense.

OBESE WILLIAM
You say something Miss?

Class laughs louder. Miss West raises a finger to her lips.

MISS WEST
Now, shush. Just ignore that.

OBESE WILLIAM
What did she say?

REBECCA
She said there's two-for-one at the drive-thru.

MISS WEST
Shush.

Jock swaps a knuckle to knuckle hand gesture with a Rebecca.

MISS WEST
I hope you're all thinking hard.

JOCK
Miss?

REBECCA
Yes Miss.

Jock and Rebecca exchange a glance.

MISS WEST
Tell us a family story. No volunteers? Rebecca.

REBECCA
Miss?

MISS WEST
Raya Baummann April 14th 1912.

REBECCA
My grandmother?
(engrossingly serious)
Aged seven; one fateful night...

EXT. TITANIC LISTING DECK NIGHT, APRIL 14TH 1912

DISTRESS FLARE explodes up in the MOONLESS SKY.

PITMAN (White-Star Officer) lowers Raya (7) into a tightly packed LIFEBOAT.

RAYA
But sir, please wait.

PITMAN
Can't wait much longer little Miss.
(to those in lifeboat)
She's the last!

RAYA
But sir, please wait.

INT. SECOND CLASS CORRIDOR NIGHT

Ankle deep in water a STEWARD checks the rooms. Passenger Yahudi wades past through the flotsam and jetsam.

YAHUDI
Let me through. Please!

He bumps the Steward.

STEWARD
Sorry, please excuse me.

Blocking his path.

STEWARD
Put your life jacket on Sir.

YAHUDI
Yes, yes I will. Thank you.

STEWARD
Life jacket on! Make your way to deck two in an orderly manner sir!
You're going the wrong way sir!

Yahudi wades on.

INT. LISTING BEDROOM NIGHT

Amongst furniture Yahudi wades amongst children's toys to a floating WOODEN CASE tagged 'RAYA BAUMMANN'.

Steward appears behind in the doorway.

Ear-water muffles the Steward's voice...

STEWARD
What are you doing? Sir! Abandon ship!

SUPERNATURAL GROAN of metal superstructure.

Yahudi grabs the Steward's 'White star' lapel and tries best he can to clamber past him.

YAHUDI
Get out of here!

STEWARD
That's what I've been trying to tell you!

EXT. A-DECK PROMENADE NIGHT

Yahudi and Steward look up to an EXPLODING FUNNEL.

Above, LIFEBOATS swing on high tension cables.

YAHUDI
It can't be.

STEWARD
She's sinking sir!

WEIRD GROAN from FALLING FUNNEL.

Yahudi trips...

From the CASE spills a TOY BEAR.

Kneeling, he stares at the familiar looking toy.

STEWARD
You went back, for a bear?

YAHUDI
You saw all the children off the boat deck?

STEWARD
All from that deck are on the Promenade sir.

Steward points to the Promenade sign.

STEWARD
That way. (beat) This way sir.

Holds his hand out to assist.

High tension cables snap!

YAHUDI
Oh my God!

Yahudi looks to the hand reaching out to him.

CABLES LASH across the deck dicing the Steward.

Seconds expand.

Averting his gaze he hears a sound like a knife through lettuce.

YAHUDI
Oh my God.

A warmth presses against and between his fingers. The red warmth is the Steward's BLOOD.

YAHUDI
Ahhh!

INT. R.M.S. CARPATHIA MAKESHIFT HOSPITAL NIGHT

Beneath blankets women and children quietly shiver or cry.

A PURSER circulates, compiling a list of survivors.

Raya receives a thermometer from a NURSE.

NURSE
You're safe now sweetheart; you're aboard the Carpathia. You look like you'll be just fine.

Glances at the thermometer and shakes it.

PURSER
The last of Boat 12.

NURSE
Not a broken bone on this one, unlike those who jumped. Not even frostbite. She insists she is Raya Bowman.

Overhearing...

RAYA
B, A, U, double-M, A, double-N.

Amends roster--

PURSER
Baummann makes seven hundred and eleven.

NURSE
Seven hundred and eleven? And the rest?

PURSER
To the eternal rest.

Shows the roster.

PURSER
One thousand five hundred dead. No celebrations here. Looks like everybody here - lost somebody.

1914 SEARCH FLARE & PRESENT DAY LANTERN - MATCH CUT:

EXT. SUBURB SCARY DARK HOUSE GATE NIGHT, PRESENT DAY

TOOTHY LANTERN held by Aliza in 'VAMPIRESS' costume and black pointy "kippa". 'BRIDE OF FRANKENSTEIN' Rebecca (white streaked hair) looks to wrist watch.

REBECCA
What ya waiting for Drac?

ALIZA
Mum said to wait here.

REBECCA
Chicken.

ALIZA
I'm not a chicken.

REBECCA
Yeah you are. Chicken, buck-buck-buck-buck. Everyone has to wake Scary Van Helsing on Halloween; trial of passage, you know how it is. Are you a man or a mouse?

ALIZA
I'm a girl.

REBECCA
Shall I get you some cheese?

Aliza opens the gate.

REBECCA
'Trick or Treat' remember?

AT THE FRONT DOOR

ALIZA
Don't knock too loudly.

REBECCA KNOCKS LOUDLY. BANG! BANG!

REBECCA
(through letterbox)
Drac's gonna kick your ass!

ALIZA
(sheepish)
Trick or Treat.

A notice on the door. "No filthy 'Junk mail', 'Halloween-ers', 'Trick or Treat-ers' or 'Carol singers'."

Slaps younger sister causing her to jump.

REBECCA
The old duffer's asking for it with all that.

Rebecca pokes an unlit FIREWORK through his letterbox.

ALIZA
No! He'll chase us!

REBECCA
He's not really Van Helsing. I reckon you can out-run him.

ALIZA
I'm scared.

REBECCA
If you stain your pants, cherish the moment. There'll be a day when you have to pay for feelings like this. Like the 'Pirates of the Caribbean ride'; think of the money I'm saving you. This is what big sisters are for.

Lighting the touch paper...

REBECCA
Old duffer! I just brought Disneyland to your doorstep!

FIZZLE and SCREAM of FIREWORK inside the house, then BANG!

REBECCA
RUN!

Aliza runs to the gate but struggles to open the rusty latch. Rebecca leaping the wall lands running.

The FRONT DOOR opens and an OLD HAND points to Aliza. SCARY VAN HELSING (97) rattles his cane up the path.

SCARY VAN HELSING
How dare you!

A CRESCENT shaped SCAR mars the old man's forehead. He reaches out snaring Aliza by the scruff of her neck; her STAR OF DAVID necklace snags in the old man's fingers.

The lantern drops at the feet of the old man.

SCARY VAN HELSING
I should have known. Filth.

FLASHBACK EXT. CITY OF OSWIECIM TRAIN STATION DAY, 1942

EICHMANN (Scary-Van-Helsing in his prime.) checks roster.

POW's disembark from a cattle train, GUARDS seemingly pull the good-looking women aside.

EICHMANN
Hungarians. Carpathian workers.
Just remember to enforce the motto.

GUARD
Arbeit macht frei! Work makes you free.

POV out of one carriage. RAYA (37, long blonde hair in a bun) shakes her hair free and frantically draws it along a sharp edge snapping it from her scalp. Her DAUGHTER (7, blonde plated ponytail) holds her mothers leg.

The CARRIAGE DOOR opens!

One GUARD pulls open Raya's coat and there hides her Daughter.

EICHMANN
Bring them both here.
(calmly)
You are?

RAYA
Baummann.

Running finger down list.

EICHMANN
Baummann.

RAYA
Raya Baummann.

EICHMANN
Yes, a Ms. Baummann.
And your daughter, yes?

The Officer feels the edge of Raya's coat.

EICHMANN
Impressive lining.

Raya looks edgy.

EICHMANN
In our workshops I expect a similar high standard Ms. Baummann. You're done here, dismissed.

Slams roster into Guard's chest.

EICHMANN
Return her daughter to the line.
(to Guard)
Next train's roster.

Snatches the roster.

EICHMANN
Just what do they expect me to do with all the Gypsies who can't work? So much filth.

INT. CAMP WORKSHOP DAY

Raya cuts patches from various materials; threads cotton through the eye of a needle and sews the first stitch between two pieces of fur.

EXT. SHOWER BLOCK DAY

Women and Children enter. One young girl is Raya's daughter.

SHOWER GUARD
Inside! All you filth must bathe!

Appearing on the scene is Raya with a patchwork BEAR in hand. A Guard holds her at arms length; another holds the door.

RAYA
She's my daughter; give it to her. Do you not have children of your own?
(calmly to daughter)
It's ok baby momma is here.

EXT./INT. SHOWER BLOCK DAY

Raya's daughter clenches a precious BEAR to her chest. The dark silhouettes of naked strangers surround her.

The door KRANGS across them all like a guillotine.

SILENCE

INT. SORTING ROOM DAY

Raya, black-eye, bruises on neck, pulls her sleeve down over a string of numbers on her wrist.

Shower Guard buttons his pants.

TRAIN GUARD
Back to work.

MOMENTS LATER

She slowly sorts through a box of what looks like hair.

The NEXT... is a blonde ponytail a mother would recognize.

Holding it to her cheek she collapses.

RAYA
No-o-o!

A patchwork BEAR lay amongst a pyramid of clothing.

CLOSE ON BEAR'S EYE: Supernaturally becoming a window to a vision of *horror*: showing the captured moment of prisoners screaming, choking and dying in the shower minutes earlier.

Raya's eyes.

INT. CAMP OFFICE SS DOCUMENT DAY

A ghostly "Auschwitz II Birkenau" stamp franks down over a map of "Oswiecim, Poland". The sound lingers then echoes away.

INT. RAYA BAUMMANN'S HOUSE BEDROOM, PRESENT DAY

Raya lifts a wet handkerchief from her eyes.

In her Diary: 'I always seem to be awakening from events of yesteryear.'

RAYA BAUMMANN 97 (V.O.)
Partisans claimed to avenge events: that's what historians would believe.
(beat)
Few survivors know the truth, which beyond any comprehension came from a force more terrifying than any heroic partisan from any ghetto.

Raya writes the Hebrew word 'Nekka'.

RAYA BAUMMANN 97 (V.O.)
Every culture hopes for justice; awakening a greater force would have one call it *revenge*.

Off-screen, Eerie TERRIFYING ROAR.

INT. EICHMANN'S DARK HOUSE CELLAR NIGHT

SNAP! A RAT twitches in a TRAP in the corner of the room.

A tearful Aliza looks up to the cellar door.

A baggy wrinkled eye peers through a circular spy hole.

EICHMANN
Cold, dark and lonely. Vermin.

Off-screen, loud banging on front door.

EICHMANN
I said no trick or treaters!

INT. DARK HOUSE FRONT DOOR NIGHT

A glowing lantern flickers through the porch glass.

Eichmann stomps his cane to the door.

EICHMANN
So... your big sis has come to brave the storm has she?

Moving the spy-hole cover aside he looks out.

The door buckles inwards; he falls, cane sliding away.

Holding his left arm, face distorting in pain. A drop of blood weals open from the crescent like scar on his forehead.

A large *shadow* crosses over him.

Regaining his feet.

EICHMANN
Yeah you'd better run! If I get my hands on you!

Reaching for the front door his knuckles whiten.

SILENCE.

He listens to a feint gentle rustling of leaves emanating from around the garden.

Behind him the house lights *flicker*.

Closing the door it slows in time.

Sound of METAL screeching.

The door clangs shut.

Then DARKNESS.

The lights *flicker* again.

Behind him, unseen; illuminated for a brief second: naked gaunt silhouettes of WWII concentration camp prisoners shoulder to shoulder, wall to wall.

Another Flicker.

He turns...

The hallway is now clear.

ELSEWHERE

EXT. SUBURB CAR (TRAVELING) NIGHT

Momma drives. Rebecca riding in the passenger seat receives a clip round the ear.

REBECCA
It was only Van Helsing's.

MOMMA
Well 'Bride of Frankenstein' you may need just a doctor when your father catches up with you. Grounded!

Rebecca shields her ear.

REBECCA
There!

She spots Aliza walking on the sidewalk, her lantern scuffs along the ground.

EXT. SUBURB SIDEWALK NIGHT

Momma cups Aliza's face, gives her a hug.

MOMMA
Are you ok honey? I'm so sorry.

Aliza smiles serenely and shows her STAR OF DAVID.

From the parked-up car Rebecca pulls faces. When Momma looks to the car she ceases.

MOMMA
Sure you're ok?

She nods.

MOMMA
I knew I shouldn't have trusted your sister. Come on honey I'll get you home.
(angrily)
I'll give her what for when I get her home.

EXT. CAR NIGHT

Behind Rebecca Momma secures Aliza into the rear seat.

MOMMA
I told you to look after your sister. And you were supposed to wait. And to not go out alone. I just don't know where you get your attitude from.

REBECCA
Check her knickers for skids.

Momma clips Rebecca's ear from the rear seat.

REBECCA
Doesn't Dracula get a bat too?

Rebecca smiles and covers her head expectantly.

EXT. MILKEN COMMUNITY HIGH SCHOOL LATE NEXT DAY

A female BULLY bumps into Aliza and swings her off her feet. STUDENTS gather.

STUDENTS
Fight! Fight! Fight!

Aliza lay on her back; the Bully closes and mounts her.

FEMALE BULLY
(tauntingly)
Are you scared?

Aliza holds her *Star of David* and watches the expectant fist rising above her face.

Enter Rebecca's large THUMPING FOOT that splits the Bully's nose open.

The Bully lay on her back with Rebecca standing over. Rebecca carries a WOODEN BOX with "REB" adorning the lid.

REBECCA
Are you scared? Yeah, thought so.

The Bully quivers. Rebecca searches the crowd.

REBECCA
See any teachers coming?

Rebecca gives the WOODEN BOX to Aliza then offers a hand to the Bully, pulling her to her feet.

REBECCA
Well, in situations like this, you have to give people a break. Hence the nose. I'm a forgiving person.

Rebecca pulls a CATAPULT off a YOUNG ONLOOKER and spits her CHEWING GUM into the loading pouch.

REBECCA
I do believe in "An eye for an eye."

REBECCA
Get running you dumb ass.

The Bully zigzags away, looking back over her shoulder.

Rebecca sees Miss West cutting through the crowd so tosses the weapon aside.

REBECCA
She must have seen you coming Miss, she ran that way!

MISS WEST
(authoritive to crowd)
Move along there's nothing to see. Go home.

Rebecca dusts down Aliza.

ON WAY HOME...

REBECCA
You'll see that hassle is the spice of life. You'll get used to it. She did have a few pounds over you.

Squeezes Aliza's biceps.

REBECCA
"Super-Fly". I do think you'd whoop anyone your own weight.

Aliza smiles.

REBECCA
About last night. I'm sorry I left you. You know I wouldn't let anyone hurt you, don't you?

Aliza nods.

EXT. SUBURB DARK HOUSE AMBULANCE STRETCHER DAY

PARAMEDICS load Eichmann into the Ambulance, his face pale, vacant, staring into infinity.

Rebecca and Aliza turn the corner of the street.

ALIZA
There's something I didn't tell you. There was something else in that house. Something much scarier.

Rebecca raises her fingers to her head like a Scout.

REBECCA
Honest Injin? Telling the truth?

Aliza raises her fingers to her head.

EXT. BAUMMANN'S HOUSEHOLD DAY

Rebecca opens the gate, runs up the path with Aliza in hot pursuit.

ALIZA
You said you wouldn't tell!

REBECCA
What? About this!

Rebecca laughs excitedly: CLATTERS in through the front door.

MOMMA (O.S.)
Girls?!

REBECCA
No, we're burglars!

REBECCA
(to Aliza)
Right, it's going to cost you this weeks allowance for me *not to tell* mom, or face the alternative; I'll get you certified and you'll have to live in an asylum and eat earwigs.

ALIZA
Oh no, Rebecca.

REBECCA
That's the spirit. Volunteer to take the garbage out and I may let you stay up an extra half hour. You got me grounded so I'm your babysitter for the night. What are big sisters for?

Aliza sulks.

REBECCA
Mum! "Super-fly" here is in big trouble! Started a fight, broke some girls nose.

ALIZA
I didn't, I didn't mum.

Door closes.

REBECCA
She did too.

MOMMA (O.S.)
That you Rebecca?

REBECCA
That's right shoot the messenger. What, you don't believe me?

INT. BATHROOM SHOWER DAY

Eyes closed Momma shampoos her hair. Her skin touches the clingy shower curtain. At the plughole blood eerily mixes with the draining foam.

Rinsing she reaches for the towel--
--through the shower curtain a GHOUL stands with her. They tangle in the clingy shower curtain.

Petrified she SCREAMS, her teeth pressing against the suffocating plastic.

Rebecca pulls the shower curtain away. Momma lay quivering, panting, her fingers curled with FEAR.

INT. EMPTY HISTORY CLASS DAY

Miss West operates a projector. The image on screen shows gaunt faces, concentration camp POW's in B&W.

Rebecca knocks upon the door and enters.

Miss West pulls the SLIDE from the machine.

REBECCA
You wished to see me Miss?

Sorting slides.

MISS WEST
Yes. Don't worry you're not in any trouble.

Miss West hands a 1945 census over.

MISS WEST
Your ancestry project?

REBECCA
I'm still working on it Miss.

MISS WEST
Well, I hope you didn't mind but I did a bit of research myself.

Opens a slim file containing a sheet "April 1945, Auschwitz liberated inmates."

MISS WEST
Know of the word genocide?

REBECCA
It's what the German's did to the Jews. Ethnic cleansing.

Miss West looks her in the eye.

REBECCA
That's what grandma says it is.

MISS WEST
Your grandma?

Miss West spins the roster round. Blue biro circles the name "BAUMMANN, RAYA".

REBECCA
That's her name.

Miss West selects a slide "Oswiecim" and drops it into the projector.

A black and white SIGN above the camp entrance reads "ARBEIT MACHT FREI".

MISS WEST
Oops wrong slide.

Taking it out--

REBECCA
--Work makes you free.

Miss West takes a seat and peers at Rebecca.

REBECCA
I know what that means.

Another slide drops into the carousel, a slide of the "Oswiecim" document with the "AUSCHWITZ" frank in red.

REBECCA
I've seen that document too.
(beat)
A dream? I don't know how.

INT. RAYA BAUMMANN'S HOUSE DINING ROOM DAY

Rebecca sits at the table. RAYA (97) makes a cup of tea in the adjacent Kitchen.

RAYA (O.S.)
How's your father?

REBECCA
He's fine. Always 'out and about'.

She brings in tea in her finest cup and saucer.

RAYA
And school? Some of your favorite biscuits.

Rebecca stares at a document, a photocopy of the "Oswiecim" roster: Raya Baummann is circled.

The cup in Raya's hand rattles.

REBECCA
Grandma?

Rebecca blinks hard.

RAYA
Help me sit down.

INT. BERLIN BAUMMANN'S TAILORS NIGHT, 1942

Raya sews a SUIT together by hand.

Pig's blood swishes across the front window. A member of the NAZI-YOUTH marks the shop front with a red Star of David.

Facing a MOB of intimidating trouble makers.

YOUTH LEADER
Your type's not wanted around here anymore that clear?

Raya looks out through the bloody window.

INT. RAYA'S BEDROOM NIGHT

Wardrobe open; clothes hang from open drawers, BEAR lay snug against the pillow.

Raya rushes around placing articles into a suitcase.

OUTSIDE a TRUCK pulls up; tailgate CLANGS, and soldier's boots hit the cobbled street.

EXT. BAUMMANN'S TAILORS NIGHT

Raya runs headlong into the outstretched arm of Eichmann. A PERSONAL ASSISTANT scrolls upon a roster.

EICHMANN
Name?

RAYA
Raya Baummann.

EICHMANN
Papers?!

Raya hands her I.D. to the Officer who waves them at the shop punctuating his dialogue.

EICHMANN
You have done well for yourself Ms. Baummann. Nice little shop, in an up and coming district. So late; where are you going in such a hurry?

Officer hands PAPERS to Assistant.

RAYA
To visit family.

The Officer nods to his ASSISTANT who ticks "Baummann, Raya - Tailor" on his roster.

EICHMANN
I'm sure we can accommodate you. Hop aboard we can pick them up en route.

Tailgate raised: an entourage of SOLDIERS accompany on foot.

INT. BERLIN MILITARY TRUCK (TRAVELING) NIGHT

Raya stands amongst a throng of claustrophobic STRANGERS.

A STRANGER stands too close, she can smell his breath.

INT. RAYA BAUMMANN'S HOUSE DINING ROOM DAY

Raya shakes, sees Rebecca touch the cup where floats a skin.

REBECCA
Cold grandma?

RAYA
Would you like another?

REBECCA
Love one. I'll make it grandma.

Raya puts her hand on Rebecca's: lost in thought...

RAYA
Rebecca? Inside you're a good girl.

INT. BERLIN BAUMMANN'S TAILORS BEDROOM DAY, 1936

Raya (31) tends to BABY ALIZA (1) in a cot.

RAYA
(whispering)
Mummy will always love you.

Bell chimes at rear of property.

RAYA BAUMMANN 97 (V.O.)
1936 was a good year. The Olympics had come to town.

INT. BAUMMANN'S TAILORS COUNTER DAY

A sporty looking BLACK MAN peers around the empty store.

BLACK MAN
Hello?

RAYA (O.S.)
Be right there.

The Black-man sniffs the air; sees the bottle of metal cleaning fluid on the counter.

Enter Raya wiping a MEDAL with a rag.

BLACK MAN
Reminds me of my sweetheart.

RAYA
Just like nail varnish aint it?

BLACK MAN
True.

Holding medal up to the light.

RAYA
Posthumous 'Iron Cross'.

BLACK MAN
Bravery. Nice gesture, one must always remember.

Sign above a rack of shoes.

BLACKMAN
"Ne sutor ultra crepidam"
(beat)
"Cobbler, stick to your last".

RAYA
You speak Latin?

BLACKMAN
Me and every 'shoe shine boy'.
(beat)
Now, just need to find a fine pair that I can run into the ground.

Raya with tape measure.

RAYA
Please take a seat Mr?

JESSE OWENS
James. James Cleveland Owens. But everyone just calls me Jesse.

RAYA
When we're done, you can leave by the front door Mr. Owens, like everyone else.

Jesse smiles.

JESSE OWENS
Much obliged Miss?

RAYA
Baummann. And you're welcome here anytime. Do please use the front door.

JESSE OWENS
Old habits.

INT. BAUMMANN'S TAILORS COUNTER DAY, LATER

Raya bites the thread off a newly made pair of trainers.

RAYA BAUMMANN 97 (O.S.)
Yeah I could say we *made* history.

EXT. BERLIN OLYMPICS BROAD JUMP DAY

A flag of five-interlocked-rings waves in the wind.

The CROWD cheers Jesse who limbers up beside the sandpit.

COMMENTATOR (O.S.)
From the United States of America, James Cleveland Owens.

In the crowd one lady kisses her marriage ring.

RUTH SOLOMON - JESSE'S WIFE
(inspirational)
Woohoo! My husband!

JESSE OWENS
(to himself)
Ruth? I hear you baby.

GERMAN MARTIAL lifts his flag from the take-off board.

GERMAN MARTIAL
Time. We don't have all day.

Jesse takes a HANDKERCHIEF from his shorts and kisses the initials R.S.

RUTH SOLOMON
Love you Jesse!

The handkerchief now rests on the floor beside the SAND PIT.

COMMENTATOR
Boldly marking the world record of twenty six feet two and a half inches.

Jesses rocks back and forth.

GERMAN MARTIAL
Last chance, boy.

RAYA BAUMMANN 97 (O.S.)
One chance is all he'd dreamed for.

MOMENTS LATER

Jesse's heels bite into the length of track.

He launches.

His heels land six inches beyond the handkerchief.

AN ELATED CROWD ERUPTS WITH GENUINE APPLAUSE!

PRESENT DAY . . .

INT. RAYA BAUMMANN'S HOUSE DINING ROOM NIGHT

Rebecca gives Raya a fresh cup of tea with biscuits.

RAYA
A few misconceptions were laid to rest that year. Germans weren't all the same.

REBECCA
(singing)
Creed and the color and the name don't matter were you there?

RAYA
I was there.
(beat)
Your History teacher?

REBECCA
Yes?

RAYA
An educated lady. There's something you should seek, one you both would find very interesting.

REBECCA
Yeah?

INT. ALIZA'S BEDROOM NIGHT

Father on Aliza's bed reads 'The Golem of Prague' fairytale.

FATHER
In Jewish folklore, there existed a magical being; neither of flesh nor blood, but made of the earth.

ALIZA
To protect the Jewish community? Miss. Ingle said that a Rabbi from Prague created a creature to protect the Jewish community.

FATHER
I and Miss Grim-tales are going to fall out big time. Doesn't she know parents have a monopoly on this kind of thing?

ALIZA
You're funny.

FATHER
Well at least Miss. Ingle aint stealing any of my funny-ness. I have a monopoly on funny-ness.

ALIZA
What does a board game have to do with funniness?

FATHER
Monopoly also means when you have something to yourself. When it's all your own. 'Mono' meaning... one, and 'poly' meaning... many. Come to think of it 'Many one' doesn't make much sense does it? It doesn't matter anyhow. You have a monopoly on cuteness.

Squeezes her cheek.

FATHER
You can count sheep? Miss. Ingle doesn't have a Cluedo about keeping secrets. Now the *Golden Fleece* was a famous sheep: one for another day. Start counting.

She giggles and cuddles into BEAR.

ALIZA
Silly. It was a lamb not a sheep.

Sighs.

FATHER
Night honey.

EXT. TITANIC CABIN NIGHT, FATHER'S NIGHTMARE

Aliza cuddles her BEAR. Twisting metal groans around her. The Cabin splits in two; air bubbles GLUG from the ship into the engulfing cold inky blackness.

Like a rag doll, a bundle of blonde hair (young Aliza) tumbles within the white water.

Tiny bubbles like sequins rise and diminish into nothingness.

White knuckles loosen from around the BEAR.

She stares up through quickly forming icy crystals.

Her pupils dilate; an icy blackness swallows the warmth, the gentle blueness of her eyes.

Motionless, her porcelain face reflects in the toy's eyes.

THEN DARKNESS

INT. PARENT'S BEDROOM DAY

Father breathes deeply: Mother gently shakes him awake.

MOMMA
Darling? Honey?

On the bedside table lay the novel "A Night to Remember", with a picture of the Titanic on the cover.

FATHER
The ship was listing, sinking. It was dreadful. So vivid. Aliza was drowning.

MOMMA
Any seven foot bears in this one? God you're a right *Di Caprio*.

FATHER
Give over, you won't tell anyone will you?

MOMMA
Destroy your street cred' would it?
Too much cheese before bedtime.

FATHER
But I love crackers.

MOMMA
You're the one who's crackers.

He tickles her beneath the sheets and they both giggle.

INT. ORTHODOX SYNAGOGUE DAY

A RABBI holds the toy bear. A secret flap shows the insides, Hebrew Scriptures. Rebecca sits patiently.

RABBI
All religious objects must be treat with respect. Large and small objects, even down to a napkin written prayer, each must be treated with the same respect. Anything with the name or spirit of God, biblical heirlooms etcetera. Ever heard of a Geniza?

REBECCA
I've seen *Raiders of the Lost Ark*. They do come smaller than that?

RABBI
Yes *The Ark of the Covenant* was a religious archive. This is Hebrew; lambskin: a passage from the Torah, the Holy Book. The writing here contains Abraham's escape from slavery in Egypt.
(beat)
Religious scriptures must be laid to rest within a specially made box, a Geniza; not destroyed.

REBECCA
I'm afraid of doing the wrong thing.

INT. MILKEN COMMUNITY HIGH SCHOOL WOODWORK CLASS DAY

A clamp holds wood at 90 degrees.

Rebecca marries it up to its mirror image creating a tube.

On a square base sits Bear.

REBECCA
(to Bear)
It's the best I could do given the time. Suppose it's up to me to bury you, do forgive me.

The tube lowers down around him.

A lid squeaks tightly closed securing Bear inside.

REBECCA
(to God)
Burning bush or lightning bolt? Anything would be helpful right now.

She writes GENIZA on the lid with a marker pen.

REBECCA
(to God)
I suppose the Commandments were left on the day's equivalent of a 'note-it', I've done my best.
(beat)
Ok, I can do better.

Picking up a chisel she carves a line...

A STAR OF DAVID slowly appears on the lid.

INT. BAUMMANN HOME NIGHT

Rebecca, Jock and Aliza all sit on separate sofas. A box of Popcorn and a Blockbuster CD rests on the occasional table.

Enter Momma and Father in evening wear. They kiss Aliza.

FATHER
(to Aliza)
Be good.

MOMMA
Take care of her.

REBECCA
I will.

Momma picks up her handbag from the table and lifts the CD: flash parental guidance sticker - (15)

MOMMA
(to Father)
A fifteen!?

REBECCA
It's a comedy.

FATHER
(to Rebecca)
You can watch it when Aliza's in bed.

REBECCA
Oh... OK.

JOCK
Yes sir.

FATHER
Night.

MOMMA
Night.

Rebecca sees her parents out; closes the door and both she and Jock relocate together on the larger sofa.

MUCH LATER

In the fetal position Aliza snoozes with her teddy. Rebecca rocks her awake.

REBECCA
Time for bed little lady.

ALIZA
(challenging)
Oh?

REBECCA
Come on. Chop chop.

A dozy Aliza picks up BEAR and climbs the stairs. She waves to Jock and he waves back.

REBECCA
Big girls brush their teeth, then I'll come tuck you in.

JOCK
(to Rebecca)
Oh that's so sweet.

Rebecca climbs the stairs, turns, mimics Aliza's cute wave to Jock and flashes her eyebrows.

REBECCA
Be right back.

Jock shovels POPCORN into his wide grin.

SOON LATER

Jock reclines with a cigar. Rebecca from the stairs--

REBECCA
--What are you doing?

JOCK
Chilling.

REBECCA
It stinks. I'm dead. I'm definitely dead. You just killed us both.

She wafts her arms in the air.

JOCK
What?

The tip of the cigar falls into the bin.

REBECCA
Pops will smell that a mile away.

In the bin the ember still burns.

Rebecca reaches into his pocket and rattles his car keys.

REBECCA
There's an aerosol that masks the smell.

JOCK
Quick ride? And Aliza?

REBECCA
Just there and back. To get the aerosol nowhere else.

JOCK
Sure.

Leaps up onto his feet.

INT. ALIZA'S BEDROOM NIGHT

Aliza sleeps. Fish swim peacefully around her AQUARIUM.

EXT. BAUMMANN HOME NIGHT

Rebecca peers to neighbor's house, tentatively locks door.

REBECCA
Straight to the store.

JOCK
Of course.

INT. BAUMMANN HOME NIGHT

The CIGAR EMBER ignites within the bin.

Moments later SMOKE BILLOWS up the stairs.

INT. ALIZA'S BEDROOM NIGHT

Aliza sleeps. Fish swim peacefully around her AQUARIUM.

ELSEWHERE IN THE NEIGHBORHOOD...

INT. COLD FLOORED KITCHEN NIGHT

MAN in boxer shorts lifts a trash bag.

Light *flickers*, he drops the rubbish; in complete darkness he steps on it.

MAN
Oh, sh#t.

Light *flickers* again.

He stands in the chest cavity of an emaciated corpse, one of many that pack the floor from wall to wall.

Not knowing where to tread, Ghoul-like arms reach up his bare legs.

MAN
Arghhh!

LIGHTS COME ON.

He stands amidst trash: no bodies in sight.

EXT. SHOP COUNTER QUEUE NIGHT

Rebecca looks at her watch. Jock juggles an Aerosol.

JOCK
The next sleep-over's at my place.

REBECCA
If it checks out with my old folks.

INT. ALIZA'S (SMOKE FILLED) BEDROOM NIGHT

Aliza clutches her pillow SCREAMING.

EXT. BAUMMANN'S HOME JOCK'S CAR NIGHT

Jock and Rebecca pull up outside.

JOCK
Hey, that your neighbor's on fire!?

At the house FLAMES lap up the LIVING ROOM curtains.

Panting, getting out of the car--

REBECCA
--No. That's mine.

RUNNING FROM THE CAR TO THE HOUSE--

REBECCA
--Nine-one-one!

Jock with CELL PHONE to ear, shakes it, looks at it.

JOCK
Come on! Gimme some reception.

Briskly gets out of the car.

JOCK
(to the street)
SOMEONE DIAL 911!

EXT. BAUMMANN HOME NIGHT

Rebecca POUNDS the door.

REBECCA
ALIZA!? COME TO THE WINDOW!

Fumbling her keys, flames cause the bedroom window to shatter.

ALIZA
(screaming)
MOMMY!?

REBECCA
GOD HELP HER PLEASE!

INT. ALIZA'S (SMOKE FILLED) BEDROOM NIGHT

Aliza coughs. The pillow falls from her arms to the floor.

EXT. BAUMMANN'S HOUSE GARDEN NIGHT

Searching the garden Rebecca frantically drops and claws at the ground. Her nails scrape at a buried box: a Star of David and the word Geniza adorn its lid.

The lid opens an inch and jams, her fingers reach frantically inside through the crack.

REBECCA
COME AWN!

In despair she SMASHES the box on the ground spilling its contents -- a TOY BEAR.

REBECCA
WHAT DO I DO?

INT. ALIZA'S BEDROOM NIGHT

Aliza's eyelids flutter. The SMOKE spiraling away under her door whistles audible words through her Star of David.

STAR OF DAVID - VOICE
A Jewish soul still yearns.

Holding her Star of David.

ALIZA
(whispering)
In my heart. I believe.

INT. BAUMMANN'S HOUSE LANDING DAY

Flames lap up the walls.

Aliza's BEDROOM DOOR - CREAKS then SPLINTERS outwards.

INT. ALIZA'S BEDROOM NIGHT

Enter a tall GHOST, that of Golyat (a seven foot simpleton)

Smoke continues to be drawn from around Aliza to his image.

STAR OF DAVID - VOICE
Hope is not yet lost.

The ghostly image quickly becomes that of a smoky seven foot BEAR made from SMOKE.

GOLYAT
MWAHHH!!

EXT. BAUMMANN HOME NIGHT

Rebecca pushes hysterically at the front door.

INT. ALIZA'S BEDROOM NIGHT

The AQUARIUM SHATTERS causing fish to flap on the carpet.

EXT. BAUMMANN HOME NIGHT

Rebecca steps back from the door and off the porch.

The front door buckles then splinters outwards.

GOLYAT
Grrraaargh!

Aliza floats three feet off the ground in a fetal position: she rests within the confines of a body of water in the shape of a bear; with fish swimming around her.

Golyat steps out of the house and onto the lawn.

Dropping to its knees the water membrane pops releasing both Aliza and several flapping fish.

Rebecca drops and gives mouth to mouth.

REBECCA
Come on. Come on, breath!

Kneeling, Jock assists.

JOCK
I did a course. You gotta let me help.

Jock assists with CPR chest compressions and Rebecca continues with the breathing.

DISTANT SIREN from Fire-Appliance and Paramedics.

REBECCA
Come on, breath.

JOCK
God please breath.

TWO PARAMEDICS crouch beside them and unpack apparatus.

FIREMAN
Is there anyone inside?

PARAMEDIC #1
Keep going you're doing the right thing.

Jock shakes his head at the Fireman.

PARAMEDIC #2
Ready, we'll take over.

Standing aside, tearful, Rebecca holds her mouth. Jock wraps his arms around her. Paramedics continue to resuscitate.

PARAMEDIC #2
Got her, she's breathing.

Aliza coughs.

Rebecca sobs with relief in Jock's arms.

JOCK
My god.

REBECCA
Save the fish.

Jock STARES at the flapping fish on the lawn.

REBECCA
(calmly)
She loves those fish.

Jock cups the fish with his hands.

INT. RAYA BAUMMANN'S HOUSE DAY

Father stands, Raya sits in her armchair.

FATHER
I know you knew the history of that bear.
I'm not leaving until you tell.

Raya pops a pill with a SHAKY HAND.

RAYA
You'll soon need these too; to sleep.
(beat)
So you wish to know about Bear?

EXT. SHOWER BLOCK DAY, 1942 (MEMORY)

Women and Children enter in single file. One crying-girl, (Raya's daughter) drags her feet.

GUARD
Get in. All are to shower!

INT. RAYA BAUMMANN'S HOUSE DAY

RAYA BAUMMANN 97 (V.O.)
I wasn't immune, I had a trade. Who'd have thought threading a needle would ever save a life; my own. Maybe if I wasn't such a coward I could have saved much more.

Cries on the back of her wrist.

EXT. SHOWER BLOCK DAY, 1942 (MEMORY)

Raya comes running with Bear in hand.

RAYA BAUMMANN 97 (V.O.)
I couldn't make things right, but I could make a toy bear.

The Guard holds her at arms length; another holds the door.

RAYA
Give it to her. She is my daughter!

INT. SHOWER BLOCK DAY

BEAR in arms; the dark silhouettes of strangers frame Raya's daughter.

RAYA BAUMMANN 97 (V.O.)
It wasn't I that had the power.

The door KRANGS across her like a guillotine.

Screams from within.

MINUTES LATER

EICHMANN
End this commotion!

GUARD
Sir we haven't inserted the poison yet.

Eichmann moves to the spy hole in the door.

Deep monstrous growl from within.

A pounding thump causes the door to buckle outwards knocking him onto his back.

Blood runs from the deep CRESCENT cut on his forehead.

EICHMANN
Drop the gas! Gas! Drop the gas NOW!

EXT. SHOWER BLOCK ROOF DAY

GUARD#1 lifts the VENTILATION HATCH. Lifts a *'ZYKLON-B'* GAS CANISTER from a WOODEN BOX.

Shrill screams from within. A deep monstrous growl shakes the shower's very foundations.

EXT./INT. HATCH/SHOWER BLOCK DAY

GUARD#2: Looks down upon the stocky dark silhouette of a seven-feet-tall patchwork BEAR.

EXT. SHOWER BLOCK ROOF DAY

Guard #1 reaches for another *'ZYKLON-B'* CANISTER and looks to the PAW holding his ankle.

GUARD #1
Aargh!

Falling, grasping the side of the BOX he and all of its contents disappear down the HATCH with an horrific scream.

INT. RAYA BAUMMANN'S HOUSE PRESENT DAY

Father rubs his hands, hairs stand erect on his arms.

FATHER
Is it me or is it chilly?

RAYA
I tell no tale. Foolishness or daring the brave to stand anywhere near the HATCH was a test of any man's mettle. It went up the ranks. The only rumor was that Hitler himself tried to stifle the truth; bad for morale so they say. Did little to stifle the Golem of Prague rumor.

FATHER
The Jewish fairy tale?

Raya shows the tattoo on her wrist.

RAYA
Jewish folklore is real; real-scary.

Father opens a hand; receives a pill and swallows.

EXT. CAMP ASH PIT DAY, 1942

LABORERS pushing wheelbarrows transport ASH to a deep pit.

An armed GUARD watches over them.

GUARD
Try not to spill it everywhere.

Raya walks sheepishly; long coat bulging to one side.

GUARD
Hey, come here!

Waves his PISTOL insinuating 'Put your hands up!'

BEAR falls from her coat to the dirt.

GUARD
Bring!

Raya takes BEAR to him.

He squeezes suspiciously.

GUARD
Smuggling?

A DAGGER plucks the stitching open.

He pulls a BLONDE PONYTAIL from within.

The PONYTAIL lands atop a mound of HOT ASH in the pit.

GUARD
Back to work.

Raya leaps onto the ASH and lifts the charred PONYTAIL like it were a lifeless baby.

INT. HOSPITAL WARD DAY

Raya lay in bed. A saline drip pokes out of her arm. A heart monitor BLIPS in an irregular manner.

Mother and Father accompany Rebecca and Aliza.

She ushers Aliza closer to the bed. Takes her hand.

RAYA
You saw my *imaginary* friend?

Aliza nods.

RAYA
And you know that adults are told to put away childish things?

ALIZA
Yes Grandma.

RAYA
Didn't tell anyone did you?

Aliza salutes with fingers to her forehead.

To Rebecca...

RAYA
You saw something too?

Rebecca bites her lip.

REBECCA
It's the bear Grandma.

Raya smiles.

RAYA
It must be put to rest. You must end this where it had all started.
(beat)
At the foot of my bed. In the Ottoman Chest...
(MORE)

INT. RAYA BAUMMANN'S HOUSE BEDROOM DAY

At the foot of the bed Rebecca and Father open the OTTOMAN.

Father lifts a DIARY.

RAYA CONTINUED (V.O.)
...amongst the old blankets.

FATHER
In a frame. She said in a frame.

Father's fingers run over the words... *A History of Bear*.

FATHER
Keep looking.

REBECCA
I'm looking.

She lifts blankets.

REBECCA
Must be this?

A PICTURE FRAME containing a dry/pressed DAISY CHAIN in the form of a ring, except missing one DAISY.

Taking the frame.

FATHER
I remember this on the wall as a kid.

Both stare at the broken DAISY CHAIN.

REBECCA
On your wall?

FATHER
Mum told us stories of the 'Wishing Tree'. I thought they were just fairy tales. The mother of all dream catchers.

REBECCA
To catch *real* monsters.

INT. HISTORY CLASS DAY

Father sits on a desk facing the front of the class.

FATHER
So, what do you think?

Reveal Miss West with the framed broken DAISY CHAIN.

MISS WEST
I suggest a field trip to Prague.

FLASH FORWARD EXT. PRAGUE LAKE DAY

A FISH rises and feeds on the lake's surface.

A TREE holds both Rebecca and Miss West's attention. In Miss West's hand hangs the broken DAISY CHAIN.

MISS WEST
Could there ever be any other tree by a lake where the fishes feed? I just hope what we're doing is right.

Rebecca plucks a vibrant yellow DAISY.

A breeze rustles the leaves high in the canopy.

Miss West walks with her arm around Rebecca. They both look back to the DAISY CHAIN swaying from a branch on -

THE WISHING TREE.

INT. HOSPITAL WARD BED DAY

Father holds Raya's hand. She exhales: quivering fingers cease to twitch.

FATHER
Mother?

Squeezing her still hand.

FATHER
Mother?

Tears.

FATHER
Do not be afraid. I'm here mum.
(beat)
If there is a God...

A supernatural LIGHT at the foot of the bed makes his head turn; a GHOSTLY GIRL appearing for but a moment.

A heavenly light from Raya's fingers comes through his hand and spreads across her whole body.

Her GLOWING SOUL she sits up, then turns and SMILES to him.

FATHER
Mother?

She floats ethereally; morphing into a vibrant Raya aged 29.

The Ghostly-girl appears again, now a little clearer.

GHOSTLY GIRL - WWII DAUGHTER
Momma?

Raya cups her lost daughter's face.

ETHERIC RAYA AGED 29
You are so beautiful.

Their essence brightens.

RAYA
(acknowledging Father)
This is my son.

The Ghostly-girl floats close to him; her blonde ponytail ever the more visible.

RAYA
Your brother.

She smiles, her essence diminishing, brightening, concentrating into a pin prick of light which returns to be absorbed by her mother's essence.

Raya now morphs into Raya aged 7.

ETHERIC RAYA AGED 7
You waited for me? All this time? I missed you dearly. You truly *are* my bestest friend forever.

The room darkens.

Father, alone, tearful, squeezes his dead mother's hand and kisses her forehead.

FATHER
Forever.
(beat)
Goodbye mother.
(beat)
Goodbye Golyat.
(beat)
Goodbye my sister.

INT. ALIZA'S NEW BEDROOM NIGHT

A hanging mobile casts tiny sparkly lights over Father who places a PLUSH BLACK CAT comforter against Aliza's cheek.

Aliza wakes--

ALIZA
--Awww... it's *Puddy*.
(beat)
Daddy? Are you letting *me* be friends with *Puddy* again?

FATHER
(whispering)
Of course sweetheart.

He dims the NEW LAMP illuminating the NEW AQUARIUM.

The MOBILE above her bed casts tiny lights upon her wall:

FATHER
Night baby.

ALIZA
Night daddy.

Snuggling into her PLUSH CAT.

ALIZA
Night Puddy.

She looks up to the BRIGHTEST twinkle on her wall: a CHAI.

Father leaves her bedroom: he leaves the door ajar.

ALIZA
(sweetest of voices)
Me and *you* Puddy are gonna be bestest friends.
(beat)
Of course it will be forever.

Footnote:

CHAI - Jewish lucky charm.

HATIKVAH - Literally "The Hope" - *National Anthem of Israel.*

INT. WOODED CHURCH YARD DAY

Rebecca removes her black cloche hat and shakes free her long blonde pony. Leaves rustle around her like tiny cymbals.

Looking at her grandmother's grave she lifts and opens - A HISTORY OF BEAR...

RAYA BAUMMANN 97 (V.O.)
Many years have passed since the horrors that once plagued the concentration camp.
(beat)
Horrors beyond my wildest nightmares.
(beat)
The BEAR with no identity, the city that lost its name.
(beat)
I did often wonder how my story would sound after I was gone: I mean just who would ever believe an old woman like myself?
(beat)
But I do believe this story should not be forgotten.

FLASHBACK EXT. AUSCHWITZ DAY, 1945

An AMERICAN JEEP drives out of camp. One G.I. riding in the rear wears a CHAI ('ח) and carries a PATCHWORK BEAR, he hums the HATIKVAH.

RAYA BAUMMANN 97 (V.O.)
Everybody takes something with them.

CLOSE IN on the eyes of the bear…

FADE TO BLACK.

THE END

ALL STORIES BEGIN SOMEWHERE...

EPILOGUE EXT. HILLSIDE PRAGUE DAY

Raya (blonde haired little girl) plays in a field of Daisies.

Plucking a Daisy, she studies it, smells it.

RAYA'S MOTHER (O.S.)
YAHUDI!

Looks towards the calling voice.

Runs towards it.

INT. HOME DAY

Enter Raya, Daisy in hand.

Raya's mother in labor, blood on her face, screaming.

The screaming ceases.

MIDWIFE
A giant baby. Golyat.

Raya's father smashes furniture.

Enter YAHUDI (Rabbi).

MIDWIFE holds a bloodied baby.

RAYA'S FATHER
(grief stricken)
Take it away.

Raya watches the midwife hand YAHUDI the baby.

THE END

FADE OUT:

'I love watching the extra material on a DVD.
I get a feeling that I've learnt a little something extra.'

'The little girl with the Bear (rear cover) is my mother.'

OLD EICHMANN'S TIMESLIP ENDING

'A work of fiction where the scariest parts are based on real events.'

REBECCA'S DETENTION ENDING

'People forget that many Jews were German.'

SNOWY CHRISTMAS ENDING

A HISTORY OF FEAR

'I approached a famous German Bear manufacturer
who weren't keen on my screenplay's original title:

...SCARED STEIFF.'

- Karl Peter Smith

END CREDIT MUSIC

OLD EICHMANN'S TIMESLIP ENDING...

EXT. AUSCHWITZ TRAIN STATION 1945

A pack of long coated JEWS shuffle towards a SMOKING TOWER.

Eichmann holds his Elder visage by the scruff of the neck. Old Eichmann pulled to his feet, stands petrified.

The old man's forehead drips blood.

EICHMANN
(whisper)
I know who you are.

Peeling open the old man's hand a 'Star of David' falls.

EICHMANN
(to Guard)
Jude. Check them more thoroughly.
(to all)
Move along!

OLD EICHMANN
(frantic)
That's not mine! I'm German. I'm German!

EICHMANN
(under his breath)
Of course, an Old German Jew.

OLD EICHMANN
(frantic)
Heil Hitler.

He raises a weak arm in the classic German salute.

EICHMANN
Move along.

RAYA BAUMMANN 97 (V.O.)
A hundred years of people losing their lives had somehow worked a dark patina into the very fabric of the bear.
(beat)
Losing my only child was the greatest hurt I could ever suffer.
(beat)
Horrors would plague the camp. Unimaginable horrors beyond anyone's wildest nightmares. The bear with an aura of fear. *The History of Bear* became...
(beat)
...*A History of Fear*.

INT. CONCENTRATION CAMP BEDROOM NIGHT, NIGHTMARE

CLOSE ON: Old Eichmann and STRANGER side by side sleep.

Old Eichmann startles awake: looks at the other and SCREAMS.

WIDER SHOT: Buckles hold Eichmann to his bed.

Post mortem clamps hold the Stranger's chest wide open.

An SS surgeon holds a trowel-like blade and moves to Old Eichmann's bedside.

Reveal: A dotted line already drawn on his chest to his navel.

Eichmann SCREAMS.

THE END

REBECCA'S DETENTION ENDING

EXT. MILKEN COMMUNITY HIGH SCHOOL DETENTION DAY

Upon the board "What have I learnt today that I can apply tomorrow? *(1000 WORDS)"*

DETAINED STUDENTS write.

Rebecca's desk is full of pencil shavings. She taps a short blunt pencil against her teeth and sharpens it. Her fingers black with carbon continue to scribble away.

She stands. Paper in hand she walks to the front desk and drops it into an 'IN' tray.

The attending TEACHER (starched WHITE shirt) glances up at the CLOCK and then to Rebecca's black fingers.

TEACHER
Finished?

Tentatively unfolding Rebecca's paper reveals the image of a BEAR made up of *A History of Fear* repeated over 250 times.

TEACHER
That's impossible.

REBECCA
(softly)
As was genocide.

TEACHER
What?

REBECCA
Just saying 'Anything is possible.'

Rebecca clutching a *Star of David* makes her way out.

Turning...

REBECCA
(kindly)
Sir? See you tomorrow sir.

THE END

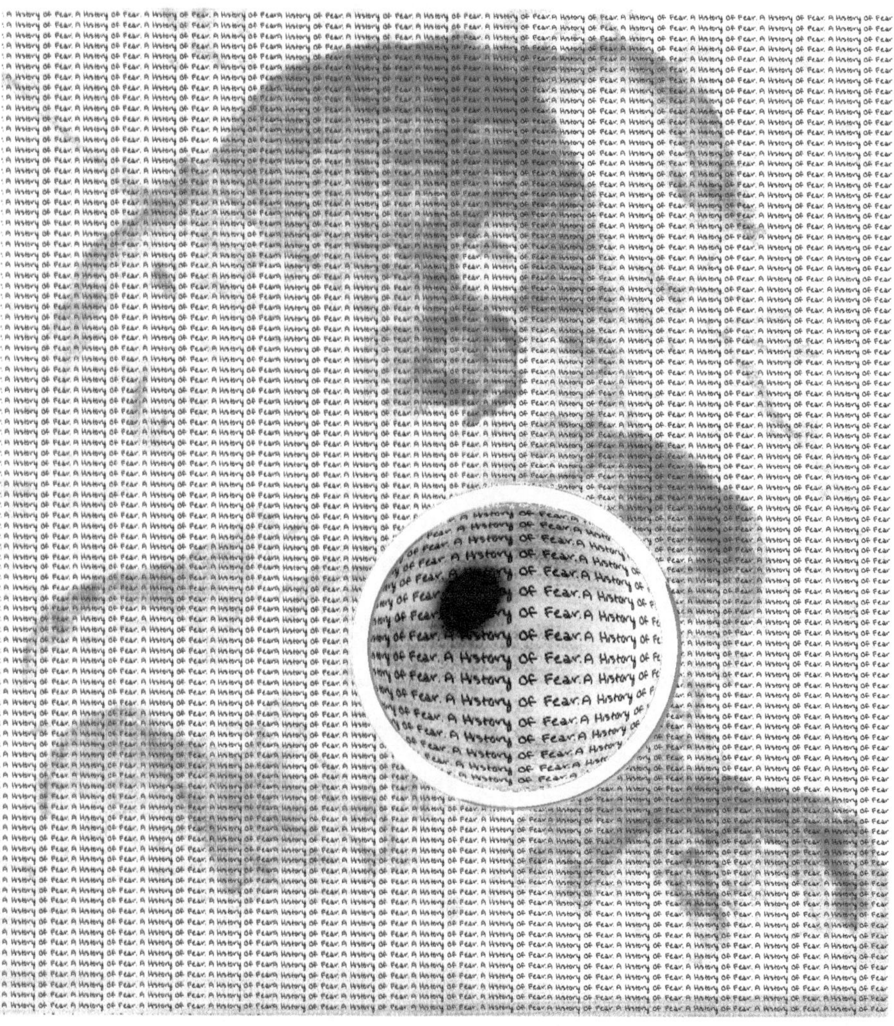
A History of Fear.

SNOWY CHRISTMAS ENDING

INT. GLENDALE GALLERIA ALLEY NIGHT (SNOWY CHRISTMAS)

A PEST CONTROLLER with shotgun lock 'n' loads.

PEST CONTROLLER
(to himself)
I saw you, you little pocket monster.

Squeaks come from inside the nearest dumpster.

Pulls out a LUMI-PAINT-GRENADE.

PEST CONTROLLER
Oh yeah, here we go, will put a bright shine on your faces.

Pulls pin, drops it through the hatch. Boom. Many SQUEAKS!

PEST CONTROLLER
Ready or not?!

Lift's lid and thumps a round blindly into the trash.

PEST CONTROLLER
Yeah, you like that?

BOOMS another round into the dumpster.

Peeking in, the TRASH glows luminous yellow.

Centimeter long footprints converge on a hole in the base.

PEST CONTROLLER
What the?

He drops to the floor; an *army* of glowing jelly-baby like creatures flees in all directions.

PEST CONTROLLER
Jesus aych!

Hastily chambers another round.

Glowing balls zigzag around the alley: some converging beneath a cardboard box.

PEST CONTROLLER
Big bad wolf to *Liddle piggies*.

BOOM! The BOX flies over the alley wall towards a NEON sign advertising a *24 HOUR FITNESS* club.

Turns to a cola can that rattles out of the darkness.

PEST CONTROLLER
Dead end boys.

It stops underfoot.

Looking out through the tiny ring-pull hole: a glowing SPRITE looks down the twin-barrels of his shotgun.

PEST CONTROLLER
Peek-a-boo!

BOOM. The can lifts into the air and over the wall.

PEST CONTROLLER
Bon voyage little freaks, don't forget to write.

Dozens of the same glowing jelly-babies appear and group in a soup of light, rising converging into a SEVEN FOOT BEAR.

PEST CONTROLLER
What the f#*^?

The glowing behemoth effortlessly scales the alley wall.

EXT. 24 HOUR FITNESS TANNING SALON ALLEYWAY NIGHT

The SEVEN FOOT GLOWING BEAR comes over the alley wall. A HOBO lifts a bottle of LIQUOR to his lips and watches it land and break into a thousand fireflies that buzz into the air and disappear amidst the twinkling stars.

Pest Controller comes over the same wall holding a shotgun.

The Wino stumbles away best he can.

HOBO
It's the *Glendale fuzz*!
Run for the hills!

INT. GLENDALE POLICE DEPARTMENT FRONT DESK NIGHT

The Pest Controller shows a doodle of a BEAR.

A HOOKER in cuffs listens in.

DESK OFFICER licks the tip of his pen, leans forwards and sniffs Pest Controller.

PEST CONTROLLER
Just which part don't you believe?

DESK OFFICER
Run this by me again. Seven foot and glowing?
(seriously)
Did it fall from Santa's sleigh sir?

The Hooker sniggers and rubs her nose.

DESK OFFICER
Wasn't a gang member?
Never assaulted you?
Or was selling narcotics?

Picks up internal telephone.

DESK OFFICER
Let me just call lost property.

Shielding telephone.

DESK OFFICER
I've got another one.

THE END

END CREDIT MUSIC

ARTIST: Killswitch Engage:
As Daylight Dies.
"THIS IS MY CURSE!"

"Will you wait for me?
Still I want,
still I ache,
but still I wait...
... TO SEE YOU AGAIN!"

A HISTORY OF FEAR
"Fairy-tale/horror."

FADE OUT

'A song to summarize my story.'
-Karl Peter Smith

'The source of the name Baummann...

My great-great auntie Cora was born Cora Jones Walters 7,30pm March 22nd, 1901. I may have been no more than 10 years old when I first spoke to her on the telephone in the 1980's. That was the only time I ever spoke to her. Thirty years on... I read her precious little Diary, a record of all the birthdays of close family and friends. A 1901 England Census records Cora's grandfather as being Christopher Bammann aged 75. In 1891 his name was spelt Bauman and in 1881 as Bowman. He was born in Mosbach, Germany about 1825.

My father's father was German and on my mother's side "Cora's story" also proves I have German ancestry going back into the 1800's. I'm probably more German, more eligible to be classed as more Arian than most SS Officers of WWII.

A lot of German Jews were more Arian by ancestry than their persecutors.

The story of two Germans; one Jewish, the other an SS Officer.

Search for Eurydice

(uri-dee-chee)

SEARCH FOR EURYDICE

GREEK TRAGEDY

Screenplay and Graphic Novel by KARL SMITH

"The most famous Orphic tale"

Two GODS wager on whether one man can succeed in the present ...and rescue his wife from the Underworld

... she's not quite dead yet!

ARGONAUTS once searched for ..."THE GOLDEN FLEECE"

Their SEARCH continues...

- Orpheus

HERMES Vs. APHRODITE

Based upon the most famous Orphic tale: SEARCH FOR EURYDICE

Screenplay & Graphic Novel

KARL SMITH

Screenplay

2 in 1

OF MEN AND MYTH

Graphic Novel

(STORYBOARD)

SCREENPLAY & GRAPHIC NOVEL

"If you completely storyboard a movie you neuter possibilities for happy accidents"
- Gore Verbinski, *Director of Pirates of the Caribbean: Curse of the Black Pearl.*

A story that will appeal to general readers and classicists alike.

When the reputations of two gods hinge on the actions of one man expect all hell to break loose when gun-toting Argonauts descend all-guns-blazing to the Underworld.

Orpheus's wife is not quite dead yet!

He must find her.

"Clutching my sister, heavy, dead in my arms; my cries for help drowned out by the music of the Pool hall. One Greek hero had been here before me; Orpheus."
- Karl Peter Smith, *The Author*.

email: orphichouse@yahoo.co.uk — titles available from all good book stores

Greek mythology
Comic book, strips
Graphic Novels

FICTION

SEARCH FOR EURYDICE:
SCREENPLAY AND GRAPHIC NOVEL

HARDBACK
ISBN 978-0-9566156-6-4

PAPERBACK
ISBN 978-0-9566156-0-2

BOOK SIZE: US LETTER 8"x11.5"

KARL SMITH

"ENJOYABLE LAUGH-OUT-LOUD!"

SPAGHETTI WESTERN FICTION

KARL SMITH

MARIN COUNTY, CALIFORNIA 1876

A YOUNG ARTIST creates a Wild West diorama and tells the seriously tall tale of NAKED SPURS, his great-great grandfather.

NAKED SPURS

screenplay

Serial Pool Attendant
SCREENPLAY
WRITTEN BY KARL SMITH
Alexandra Vino
Brian Spangler
TV PILOT & SERIES BIBLE
Keeping L.A. clean is just MURDER.
* Includes the 24 PAGE 'Bible' for the TV Series. L.A. Serial Pool
A minute by minute breakdown of the 'Hero's Journey' for TV.
(p.84-107.)
Four-Act Structure, where Act breaks match commercial breaks.
An insight into ABC, CBS, NBC, FOX, and new BBC TV format.
Serial Pool

SERIAL POOL ATTENDANT

Synopsis:
On an L.A. beach Alex (pool attendant) meets her idol, the notorious Shark (real name Henry, a high profile killer on parole). Shark mentors Alex in the art of 'murder' and in 'not getting caught'. Cultural references lead to his catchphrase . . .

"A CLASSIC!"

The big reveal: Shark is not just a serial killer but a puppet taking orders from Victoria (once screenplay tutor to Alex) and mission director of an assassin-like organisation known as the . . .

'SERIAL POOL'

It is not mere chance that brings Alex and Henry together.

Siblings with a flair for death. Shark takes his sister under his wing.

Hitmen liaising as *real CLEANERS.*

"IF YOUR PROBLEM IS TOO BIG TO FILTER . . .YOU CALL THE POOL ATTENDANT"

Concept:
Two loyal Psycho's team up to create the L.A. version of "Miami Vice". Add a sexy mission director... Victoria... a sprinkling of "Mission Impossible" and that's ENTERTAINMENT!

"YOU'LL DIE LAUGHING"

"...lunatic brother-sister psychology at its finest."

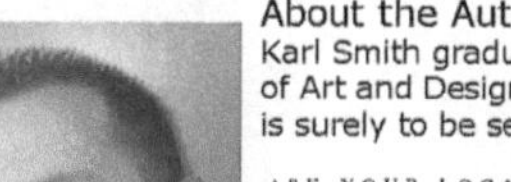

About the Author
Karl Smith graduated with a degree in Fine Art from Cleveland College of Art and Design. His fresh fusion of action and emotion when screenwriting is surely to be seen in a cinema near you soon. Bet your mortgage on it!

ASK YOUR LOCAL BOOK STORE TO STOCK OTHER ORPHIC HOUSE TITLES

SERIAL POOL ATTENDANT: SCREENPLAY & TV SERIES BIBLE

HARDBACK
ISBN 978-0-9566156-7-1

PAPERBACK
ISBN 978-0-9566156-2-6

Purge
the Soul
screenplay
written by
KARL SMITH

step on

HOLY GROUND...

...AND THEY'LL BURN FOR THEIR SINS

from the HEAVENS

a ***FALLEN ANGEL***

from MOUNT CALVARY

the ***ROMAN*** *who speared CHRIST*

their FINAL DESTINATION

the

' SCALA SANCTA '

HOLY STAIRS

THE VATICAN CITY

to save the ***POPE*** *from ASSASSINATION*

About the Author

Karl Smith graduated with a degree in Fine Art from Cleveland College of Art and Design. His fresh fusion of action and emotion when screenwriting is surely to be seen in a cinema near you soon. Bet your mortgage on it!

PURGE THE SOUL:
SCREENPLAY

PAPERBACK

ISBN: 978-0-9566156-5-7

Christianity

Screenplay

France/Italy

FICTI

COMING SOON

Memoirs of Dirty Max
Screenplay
written by
Karl Smith

The up-curve of an affair is sex.

Max either 'gets off' quickly or puts his hands in the air and 'enjoys the ride!'.

Between ROLY-POLY and ROMP he may just find . . .
. . . his fairy-tale ROMANCE.

For fans of *Alfie, Hitch* and *Hung.*

A TRUE STORY

About the Author
Karl Smith graduated with a degree in Fine Art from Cleveland College of Art and Design. His fresh fusion of action and emotion when screenwriting is surely to be seen in a cinema near you soon. Bet your mortgage on it!

ASK YOUR LOCAL BOOK STORE TO STOCK OTHER ORPHIC HOUSE TITLES

MEMOIRS OF DIRTY MAX:
SCREENPLAY

PAPERBACK
ISBN: 978-0-9566156-4-0

United Kingdom
Screenplay
Romance
FICTIO

COMING SOON

'Moving words around a page is like painting.'
To learn this process check out... Print-on-demand Technical Guide: Screenplay Publishing

Screenplay Resume | Artwork

Karl Peter Smith

E-PORTFOLIO:
1. Search for Eurydice - Romance with Bite
2. Serial Pool Attendant - Crime
3. Naked Spurs - Western
4. A History of Fear - Horror
5. Purge the Soul – Thriller
6. Memoirs of Dirty Max - Romance
7. Bikini THREE-20 (Thunderbirds) – Sci-Fi
8. Bill and Ted's Idiot's Guide to Screenwriting - Comedy

EDUCATION
UNIVERSITY OF TEESSIDE, Cleveland, England.
Bachelor of Fine Art - Printing, Drawing and Painting.
Specialized in Sculpture

HONOURS
Cleveland College of Art and Design used my sculptures to advertise the college in the UCAS prospectus; a national publication attracting future students to campus.

"I cried whilst writing."
A History Of Fear
"...the blonde ponytail."

Thanks Helen x

Pencil Drawing of Miss. Helen Shepley by K.S. 2006

To My Loving Family
enclosed...
the History of Bear.
...a History of Fear
TAG DER VERPFLICHTUNG DER JUGEND 1943
DEUTSCHES REICH

www.ingramcontent.com/pod-product-compliance
Lightning Source LLC
Chambersburg PA
CBHW030814310726
48980CB00006B/487/J

* 9 7 8 0 9 5 6 6 1 5 6 9 5 *